Umang

Every Cloud has a Silver Lining

"Umang- Every Cloud has a Silver Lining"

ISBN No: " 978-93-90799-59-6"
1st Edition
Language – English and Hindi

Flairs and Glairs
Publication House
Regd. Under MSME Act.

Disclaimer

This is a work of fiction and solely represent the thoughts of the corresponding authors of the articles. Our editors have tried their best to edit the content of all the authors and check the plagiarism.
All the write-ups in this book are unique and are only published in this book.
In case any plagiarism or error is found, only the author is responsible alone, and not the publisher or the Compilers.

Cover Designing and Book Formatting
Shubham Shah and Ishani Agarwal

Acknowledgement

I would like to thank my family and my soulmate for everything. I don't think without your support, anything would have been possible for me.

Founder, Shubham Shah sir and co-founder Ishani mam you are very friendly and helpful. You always solved my queries and the kind hearted Ms. Shivangi Jaiswal di as a project head, you helped me a lot in my journey of compilation. Thanks to the whole team "Flairs & Glairs" for giving me a chance to represent such a nice topic "Umang ".

Last but not least, my appreciation goes to all my Co-authors. Without your love, support and help this was not going to possible for me to compile this beautiful anthology. Thank you for helping me, in the journey of "Umang" by being so patient and completing our book in such a short time!

Co Author

Shubham Shah (Founder Flairs and Glairs)
Ishani Agarwal (Co-Founder Flairs and Glairs)

1. Shivani Sarwade (Compiler)
2. Abhay Rakhunde
3. Aishwarya Umashankar
4. Ajay Poddar
5. Ankeeta Sahani
6. Anwesha Patra
7. Avi Srivastava
8. Bhakti Patil
9. Chandni Kesharwani
10. Deepjyoti Chowdhury
11. Diksha Motwani
12. Ganesh Patil
13. Gauri Kondane
14. Gautam Saini
15. Guneev
16. Harshvardhan Gupta
17. Hema Kirthiga J
18. Ishita Tiwari
19. Ishrat Jahan Noormohammed Khan
20. Ishrat Saboon
21. Jayashree Sahoo
22. Kalamkaar
23. Karan Nishad
24. Keerthana Suriya
25. Krinjesh Maru
26. Krishna Motwani
27. Laxmi Mondal
28. Mausam Agrawal

29. Mohanapriya K
30. Om Prakash Lovevanshi
31. Pragya Verma
32. Pragyan Panda
33. Prasad Babu Galla
34. Pratik Jadhav
35. Punita Sinha
36. Rahul Shende
37. Reena Kadam
38. Reetika Singh
39. Reshma Anwar Shaikh
40. Sahina Ghugha
41. Saumya Bhatia
42. Shazia Jabeen
43. Shivangi Patankar
44. Shivani Bhardwaj
45. Shradha Gindlani
46. Siddhi Srikrishna Kulkarni
47. Srijani Das
48. Tanmay Yadav
49. Utkarsh Devale
50. Vaishnavi Hend
51. Vinod Umratkar

Shubham Shah

(Founder- Flairs and Glairs)

Shubham Shah, an entrepreneur at "Flairs & Glairs" a brand with dynamics in events organizing and cultural educational pan INDIA, is a 26yrs old guy who recently has entered the digital platform of imprinting emotions. He has initiated with his own open mic platform to help budding poets and aspiring writers under his brand named as "Teekhe Zasbaaat"

He is a commerce graduate from the Bhagalpur City of Bihar. He states Writing has impersonated him since childhood and he has now been writing for over a decade!
Cooking, on the other hand, is his passion! He also mentions, trying out new things just tickles him!
When asked sir, Why SPICY EMOTIONS?
He smiled and added, "agar jasbaat teekhe na ho toh wo jasbaat kahan" Spices are all that blends! So do his words!
As a chef, he presents to you his dish! Hot and freshly served! Taste it! Feel it! Enjoy it! You can also find his writing in the Book "Teekhe Zasbaaat" and 50+ Co-authored anthologies. With his passion to explore opportunities across Platforms, he is working with keen devotion and We wish him all the very best for his future ventures.
He is Featured in the **International Magazine De-Mode** for his upcoming solo novel.
He is **Approved by Ne8x for its Lit Fest,** and is a **Golden Star Awards 2020 Winner.**
He is an **India Book of Records Holder** for his Anthology **Satrang,** and has the **Grandmaster** title by **Asia Book of Records**, for the same.
He has also been featured in **Prabhat Khabar**, **Dainik Jagran** and other renowned Newspaper for his achievements. He has also been awarded with **India Star Republic Award 2021.**
He has been a proud co-author to
India Book of Records (Title- Black)
World Book of Records (Title -15 Wonders of Poetries)
India Book of Records (Title - Aaina)
Vajra World Records Holder (Title - Gustakhi Maaf Hai)
High Range of Records Holder (Title - Gustakhi Maaf Hai)

Share your reviews on his

INSTAGRAM

@spicy_emotions
@shubham4shah

Or via email on

shubham2shah@gmail.com

To stay tuned to his work and opportunities follow his business Handles

INSTAGRAM FACEBOOK YOUTUBE

@flairsandglairs
@teekhezasbaaat

WEBSITE:

https://flairsandglairs.in/
https://flairsandglairs.com/

Ishani Agarwal

(Co-Founder- Flairs and Glairs)

Ishani Agarwal hails from the City of Joy, Kolkata.
She is the co-founder of her Community "Teekhe Zasbaaat" and Flairs and Glairs Publication.
Been a Compiler for 45+ Anthologies, she is in the process for more. Co-authored in 150+ Anthologies. She is a India Book of Records Holder, a Vajra World Records Holder, a High Range of Records Holder and a Bravo Record holder.

Approved by Ne8x for its Lit Fest 2020, and Literary Icon 2020. Also a Golden Star Awards Winner 2020.

She has also been awarded with India Star Republic Award 2021.

She has been featured by the National Magazine "Taree Zameen Par" with the title 'unstoppable'.

Also featured in the International Magazine DeMode for her upcoming solo novel, she is proud to write on social issues, and is happy with the love she is receiving.

Connect with her on Instagram: @Ishani_agarwal_quotes / @compilations_so_far

SHIVANI SARWADE
(Compiler)

Shivani, hailing from the city of God Vitthal, Pandharpur. She is an ambitious girl who follows her heart and loves to write what her heart says! She is a future pharmacist. She can sense God in her parents along with that believes in love, kindness and humanity too. Poetry and art of sketching is her passion. She has worked as co-author in so many anthologies. She loves to write in Marathi and Hindi especially in a simple language. Instagram handle- @shivanisarwade_

क्योंकि तुम मेरी उमंग हो

हर परीक्षा में अव्वल आती हूँ,
क्योंकि तुम मेरी उमंग हो ।

हर मुश्किलों से लढ़ती हूँ,
क्योंकि तुम मेरी उमंग हो ।

गिरकर भी बार बार खडी हो जाती हूँ,
क्योंकि तुम मेरी उमंग हो ।

मेरी आँखों में मुस्कान बनाये रखती हूँ,
क्योंकि तुम मेरी उमंग हो ।

हर तरफ तुम्हे अपनी जान कहते फिरती हूँ,
हा माँ, क्योंकि तुम ही मेरी उमंग हो ।

तू

रुखरुखत्या मनांस आधार तू
जगणं सुसह्य घडविणारा तू
निसंदेह निद्रेचे कारण तू
अबोल भावनेचा बांध तू
दुःखाचे सावट लोटणारा तू
तुजविण आयुष्य उद्ध्वस्त जणु
मुलगा, भाऊ, बाप तू
वेड्या राधिकेचा कृष्ण तू
इवल्याशा जीवाचं जगणं तू
प्रेमळ नात्याचं स्वागत तू
प्रत्येक जबाबदारीचा सांभाळ तू
अर्धांगिनीच्या चेहऱ्यावरची खळी तू
मातेच्या वात्सल्याचा आनंद तू
सर्वांची मने जपणारा तू
परंतु स्वहित न जाणणारा तू
फक्त तू आणि तू.

ABHAY RAKHUNDE

This journey is not easy. It's not about the words it's all about emotions. Some are exposed, some are forgotten. He is not a professional writer. He simply writes his emotions on paper; the people call them poetry. He started writing as time pass but mean time he enjoyed this.

मी तू

मी शब्द विखुरलेले चोहीकडे
तू पद्धतशीर ठेवणीची आकडेमोड
मी स्वतःत गुरफटलेला धागा
तू सरळ तलम रेशम बिनजोड

मी अतरंगी विदूषक स्वच्छंदी
तू शिस्तप्रिय तलवारीची धार
मज पायी फिरे भोवरा गरगर
तू सांजेला घर शोधणारी घार

मज उकल दे सये या पटलावरी
सांग तूझ्या माझ्यात अंतर का मैलांचे
अन् सुटत नाही हे ही गणित
चालती चार पदके परंतू ठसे दोन पावलांचे

AISHWARYA UMASHANKAR

An enthusiastic person with a positive spirit towards everything. Hailing from Tamilnadu with a vision to experience, enjoy and succeed in every task taken. Lives with a moto 'Short life with a big world to enjoy. Hence Never accept anything low’. Rising with love for world and nature and blooming in the form of poetries at her Instagram handle @__uv_says. Here’s the one from the bottom of her heart to reiterate the real happiness we all bore once. May this bring in better sunshine to the readers' life and kindle positivity.

Real essence of enthusiasm

Kick started the story from a dark room
when tears could reap happiness too.
Single cry partitioned life and doom
then began the era of me and you.
People and pains unknown
just crawling around the area with grin.
Hearing wondrous music of lullaby and retorting cooing tone
thereby grasping every attention and finding kin.
With no bias and judgements
With eyes that shows only enthusiasm
owning and showering contentment.
As maturity hits hard making a chasm
it taught the knowledge of right and wrong.
The innocence and positive spirits are all gone.
But remember to carry the child in you all along!
Feel and protect it always.
Hence ask the child the road to joy and enthusiasm
And visualize the real essence of happiness in its eyes!

AJAY PODDAR

He is Ajay Poddar 'Anmol' from Kolkata, mainly his most of works started from Uttarakhand he used to live in Madhya Pradesh he is the only person in his family who loves literature because he thinks only literature and positive literacy can change the world and society after 7 years of struggle, he entered in literature fully by professional development from dream analysis,

He wants to proof that universal fact literature is directly proportional to science and science is directly proportional to god and god is directly proportional to literature.

'अनमोल' अजय पोद्दार हूँ मैं

अपनी ही गुजरती जिंदगी का सार हूँ मैं,
अगर समझो तो 'अनमोल' हूँ अनयथा अंगार हूँ मैं,
मिटा नहीं कोशिश हजार की लोगो ने,
माँ का आशीष लिए पिता का सम्मान हूँ मैं,
मिट्टी का पुतला हूँ मिट्टी में मिलना है मुझे,
बेतहाशा हर दिल में बेशक खिलना है मुझे,
हिंदुत्व रक्षक डमरू की पुकार हूँ मैं,
मातृ हिंदी का अलंकार हूँ मैं,
साहित्य को राग में लिए संगीत का श्रृंगार हूँ मैं,
बंसी की मधुर ध्वनि सुदर्शन की ललकार हूँ मैं,
वीणा के रिदम का सार हूँ मैं,
पुष्पित हूँ गुरु के चरणों में,
मित्रों की मर्यादित वास्तविकता का आधार हूँ मैं,
हृदय से स्व-स्वप्न सँजो दूँ उसी स्वप्न रक्षा का यलगार हूँ मैं,
कलम मेरा शस्त्र स्याही का परम यार हूँ मैं,
छोटा बेटा हूँ हिंदी माँ का परिचय से 'अनमोल' अजय पोद्दार हूँ मैं,
सचेत प्रेम का सीधा सादा सा जीर्णोद्धार हूँ मैं

ANKEETA SAHANI

Ankeeta Sahani
09.09.2001
Hirakud/Odisha
Content Writer, Radio Jockey, Actor, Program Host.
IG/Fb: @ankeetaas
Mail Id: ommsri242@gmail.com

किनारा

मैं बहुधा बहा लेती हूं अपने आप को
पीड़ा बहती उस नदी के बहाव में...
यही सोच कर, की हो सकता है
इस दर्द का भी कोई न कोई
किनारा अवश्य ही होगा ।

ANWESHA PATRA

Anwesha Patra is a 16-year-old science student and being a teenager with raging emotions inside her, she converts them into forms of poetry, to calm herself down, and also posts them on her social media @__.the_paperwinged__ so that other people can read and relate to themselves too. :) And at the end of her poems, she likes to mention her name in her mother tongue, bengali.

I PITY MYSELF

I pity myself,
For being a loser.
I pity myself,
For being completely useless
Even after seeing him in pain.
I pity myself,
For I cannot move...
Even If I want to.
Extending my arms,
But they're too short,
Trying to outrun the distance,
But it's infinite.
I pity myself,
For all I can do is pray and cry.
Consoling myself by
Hoping that one day,
It'll all be fine....
I pity myself,
For being a loser...
But how far can I go...
Is a question yet left to answer......

AVI SRIVASTAVA

He is an engineering student aimed to make his name in computer world. Poetry is not only is his hobby but also a way to express his feelings.
Instagram Id: Avishri99

हो सकता हैं प्यार दोबारा

टूटा चुका था मैं एकदम, गिर रहे थे आंसू झरझर....
करता था बेइंतिहा मोहब्बत में जिससे, छोड़ गई वो मुझे बीच मंझदार पर....
समझ नही आ रहा था, क्या करूँ किधर जाऊँ....
खुशहाल जीवन का ढोंग करूँ या फिर मर जाऊँ....

जूझ रहे थे असमंजस से हम, तब मिला एक दोस्त का सहारा....
उसकी बातों ने किया ऐसा असर, जैसे डूबती कश्ती को मिला किनारा....
रोज़ करता उससे बातें, बाट लेता दिल के सारे गम....
खोने लगे हम ख्यालो में उसके, एक अनोखे एहसास ने लिया था जन्म....

फिर पड़ रहे थे हम उसी झमेले में, जिससे उभरने में लगा था इतना वक़्त....
वो अनचाहे से जज्बात, मेरे मन में देने लगे थे दस्तक....
मेरे पहले प्यार में थी कमी कोई, शायद इसलिए टूट गया था रिश्ता हमारा....
ऊपर वाले कि माया कहूँ या दिल की जरूरत, हो गया हमें भी प्यार दुबारा....

पत्ती हूँ मैं

सूख चुकी हूँ मैं लेकिन पहचान मेरी आज भी वही हैं....
जिस मिट्टी से जन्मी थी मुझे दफन होना वही हैं....
कहने को हूँ में पेड़ की अमानत पर जब तक उससे जुड़ी हूँ....
जिन पत्तियों की छाया ढूंढते हैं लोग आज उनके लिए अंखिया बिछाये बैठी हूँ....

याद हैं मुझे आज भी वो खुशी जो मेरे निकले पर लोगो को होती थी....
लग जाते मेरे बचाव में हर वक़्त एहमियत मेरी इतनी होती थी....
नन्हे पौधे से पेड़ बनी थी में मेहनत सफल करके तेरी....
आज झड़ गई हूँ में पूरी तो खत्म हो गई कद्र मेरी....

BHAKTI PATIL

या भक्ती हिंदुराव पाटील आहेत. ज्या राधानगरी(कोल्हापूर)च्या असून, लिखित काव्यप्रमाणेच साहित्यामध्ये यांत्रिक एकोप्या ऐवजी जैविक ऐकोपा अच्युत पध्दतीने साधतात. ज्या सध्या नवपदवीधारणा नंतर साहित्याला अत्युच्च साकारण्यास प्रयत्नशील आहेत.

हे नववर्षा

भीतीच्या पल्याड, अंधार छेडल,
ऊर्जेचा दिस उजडेल असा सूर्य तू घेऊन ये ||

भूतकळच्या पुसुनी चुका, भविष्याच्या स्वप्नांना मारण्यास हाका,
भरारीचे पंख घेऊन ये ||

सुखाच पडू दे चांदण, फुलुदे आयुष्याचे अंगण
असा आनंदी पाऊस घेऊन ये ||

अंधारातल्या राक्षस भीतीचा, दिसाच्या देव संगतीचा माणूस जरा निरखून घे ||

भावनिकता सांडून, व्यवहारी खेळ मांडून
लोभी जगात स्वतःला सुरक्षित कोंडून घे ||

घेऊन ये विकास तारे, विझवुनी टाक आक्रोशाचे निखारे, फुलवण्यास नव्याने दे शौर्याचे अंगारे ||

आयुष्याच्या गाठोड्याला, फाटक्या
सुतलीळा, उमेदीच नवं ठिगळ विणून घे ||

हे नववर्षा येताना थोडी ओंजळभर आशा घेऊन ये जगण्यास नवी अभिलाषा रुझवून दे ||

CHANDNI KESHARWANI

An entrepreneur by profession Chandni Kesharwani holds Masters of Child Psychology. She feels privileged to live in different cities around the world and that gave her opportunity to make friends from all walks of life and different nationalities. She wants to establish as a motivational poet and writer. Presently she is very active on social media platforms and her motivational quotes on life have been liked by many people. She has written two anthologies before. She presently lives in Gurgaon, Haryana. Instagram - @hindi_sahityakar
E mail: chandni.kesharwani1981@gmail.com

शहरी सजना

शहर को जाईके,
सूट पहिन के,
चश्मा टाई लगावत।
दूध और दही,
सब छोडत सजना,
बस कॉफी मग उठावत ।
अब सजन मोरा
हबी होई गवा ।
गुड़ चना मोहे वापस दइके,
मुर्गा टांग मगावत ।
दूध मलाई न खावत सजना,
वह तो वोडका घूंट लगावत ।
अब सजन मोरा
हबी होइ गवा ।
घुंघट पल्लू मोरे साड़ी का ,
अब ना उसको
सुहावत,
अंग्रेजी के बोल
बोलकर,
मॉडर्न ड्रेस पहनावत।
अब सजन मोरा
हबी होई गवा ।

DEEPJYOTI CHOWDHURY

Deepjyoti Chowdhury embraces reading and writing as her escape from the real world as well as a window to it. She is a strong believer of Christ and Karma. Currently pursuing Master's in English literature, she has written in 100+ anthologies, she is the author of "Heartfelt musings" and "The staircase to freedom". Her main aim is to heal people and make them smile through her art of writing.
You can follow her on Instagram at @dj_writes_to_heal

THE ALMIGHTY

Before praying, insightful of my wishes;
He is marvelous, I am His witness.
What He begins, He certainly finishes;
Has in store all the heavenly riches.

House of truthful men He flourishes,
We praise Him by worship and services.
He is gladdened by rightful practices,
He heals every hazardous sickness.

His mercy and grace are limitless,
He loves unconditionally, regardless.
He calms the mind and soul that's restless,
He welcomes us with both arms stretched.

The bleeding and hurtful souls he touches,
Removes every evil and wicked forces.
Our dark and void life he lightens,
Filling our souls with righteousness.

DIKSHA MOTWANI

Diksha is a passionate girl from Mumbai, Maharashtra. She loves to pen her feelings. She is introvert but her pen makes her extrovert. She is a writer, singer, artist and a poet!

Still am waiting!

You promised that you will be back very soon,
But you didn’t,
I attempted to forget you as you were may be a boon,
But I didn’t!

Yes, you are still my morning's first thought,
Yes, I still adore you,
Yes, I still love you.
But may be now, I will not have you.

You were my blooming moon,
You were my shine of darkest days,
unfortunately, you are not mine now,
Yet I still wait for you every single day!

GANESH PATIL

This is Ganesh Sadashiv Patil. He is the student of UG in field of pharmacy. He has writer and poet who writes 50+ poetry in Hindi and Marathi languages. He loves to write on love, humanity, motivation and social themes. He loves to write down his feelings, his thoughts on various topics which makes him a writer of one his own kind. He likes to express the life in words of poetry. He is coauthor of the book जिक्र-ए-जज्बात 2.0.

जीवन

जीवन का बस एक यही उद्देश है सबको यहा हमे खुश रखना है
कोई ना हो मायूस यहापर हमसे ना किसीओ करना मायूस हमे है
सुख हर एक को हमे देना है दुःख ना किसिके जीवन में लाना है
हर एक को मिले यहा खुशी बस इसी बात पर हमे गौर करना है
आचरण ये हमारा अच्छा रखना है ना किसिसे हमे बेहस करना है
योग्यअयोग्य का ध्यान रखकर हमे आगे मंजिल पर बढते जाना है
स्वार्थ से भरे मन को हमें काबू में रखना है ना इसे बिछडणे देना है
निस्वार्थी मन से कर के सेवा यहा हमे जिंदगी में बस खुश रेहना है
नफरते ना यहा हमे बढने देनी है प्यार की भाषा को हि सिखलाना है
हरएक रहे संग मिलकर यहा बस इसी बात पर हमे ध्यान रखना है
ये जीवन तो मिलता बस एक ही बार है हमे इसे आदर्श जो बनाना है
जिवन के हर एक लक्ष को पार यहा करके हमे आगे बढते जाना है

Quotes on Life

1) I started with nothing now I stop for nothing

2) Never give up because great things take time

3) No one has ever achieved greatness by playing it safe

4) Never forget who helped you in the hardest time

5) Inside a person you know there is a person you don't know

6) You can judge me or fight me but you can never stop me

GAURI KONDANE

She is Gauri. She has completed her BE and recently pursuing M.Tech. Basically she is an endless reader. Loves the rain(pluviophile).

Not writer by profession it is just a way of express feelings.

Umang tere aane ki

Mere yaadon ke andhere ko
Roshni se mitane ke liye
Tere aane ki ek umang hi kaafi hai....

Udaas rehne wale mere chehre ko
Hasi se khilkhilane ke liye
Tere aane ki ek umang hi kaafi hai....

Intezaar me jhuki meri nazaro ko
Umeed se chamakne ke liye
Tere aane ki ek umang hi kaafi hai....

Bejaan pade mere is jism me
Jeene ki khwaish Jagane ke liye
Tere aane ki ek umang hi kaafi hai....

GAUTAM SAINI

Gautam Saini is from Karnal, Haryana. He currently opts medicine as academics and running Instagram page @the_writerdesk. He is a Gold medalist in Science Olympiad and 2nd Runner up in KOCA (World's Biggest Youth fest). He loves to do writing, acting, vlogging, teaching, singing. He writes because he felt that it is the best way to explore ourself and it makes him remind of halcyon days.

एक तस्वीर

एक संदूक मिला पुराना सा,
मिट्टी में मैला सा।
कभी देखा तो नहीं था घर में, पर अपना सा लगता था।
खोला उसे तो तस्वीर मिली पुरानी सी,
पहली बार में पहचान ना आयी एक छोटी सी बच्ची प्यारी सी।
एक आवाज़ कमरे से आयी "मै तुम्हे सब बताती हूं"
देखा जो गर्दन फेर कर कमरा तो बिल्कुल खाली था।
तस्वीर जो हाथ में थी वो ही बोल उठी थी।
उसने कहा !!
देख रहे हो जिसको तुम वो अम्मी जान तुम्हारी है,
और ये बात कुछ 50 साल पुरानी है।
जब तुम्हारी मां भी पढ़ा करती थी,
बड़े अफसर बनने के सपने देखा करती थी।
तस्वीर में जो तुम झांक रहे हो,
माई को नासमझ आंक रहे हो।
वो तो तुम्हारे नाना ने बेड़ियों में उनको बांध दिया था,
जब से तुम्हारे पिता जी ने शादी का नाम लिया था।
तुम्हारे खातिर जिसने अपने ख़्वाब सारे छोड़ दिए,
उसको भी पसंद था जीना खैर इन सब से मुंह मोड़ दिए।
फुर्सत के हर पल वो तुम पर वार देती है,
अपने लिए नहीं बस तुम्हारे लिए ही जीती है।
अगर वो आज अपने लिए जीती तो,
सवाल कई बनाए जाते, शायद तभी तुम उसकी अहमियत को समझ पाते।
अब जिसके सारे ख्वाब अब तुम में ही जीया करते है,
शाम होते ही जिसके नैन तुम्हे देखने को तरसते है।
कभी उसे भी लेट तक सोने दिया करो,
अपने आप में खोने दिया करो।

कभी बनो छांव सा उसके लिए धूप में,
ढल जाओ जैसा चाहती है मां उस रूप में।
अब तुम भी तस्वीर के बोलने से पहले ही समझ लेना,
बैठ कर मां के पास दिल के सारे राज़ खोल देना।

GUNEEV

Guneev is a budding writer and poet (14 years old). Being an ardent reader, she loves to jot everything and anything. Participating in various competitions gives her motivation to do better.

Tours!

I love to travel
That too, more in my dreams
Where the roads are endless
And routes infinite.
Millions of friends I make
With no one to get aggressive or scold

Finding it my own
By not being a traveller
No day, no night
Just ecstasy and fun!!
I wave out how to love the world
After witnessing myself
In changing skies

From Rome to Mars
Everywhere I travel
Yet most of the times
In my new world :
"GEMLIFE"
With cites digital
And everything electric and smart
Peeps in search of nothing
But everything

In my quotidian life,
I fly in aeroplanes
I sail in boats
And what not?
Everything that appeals me
And gives me a sooth at the core

Learning is even there
Libraries, restaurants and even schools endless
Discovering my own paths
Trying to become the next Edison or Newton
Yet I dream
And I dream
In the hope of transforming dream to reality

LEARN, EXPLORE AND DISCOVER!

HARSHVARDHAN GUPTA

Harshvardhan is a student of computer engineering in 2nd year diploma and is working hard for his education as well as for his passion. He is passionate in writing thoughts, quotes, poetry, anthology and many more, just what writers do. He wants to spread positivity and motivation through his words, so that people can stay happy.

मोहब्बत की गलियों से हर वक़्त गुजर जाऊँगा

मोहब्बत की गलियों से हर वक़्त गुजर जाऊँगा
ना दिखे मुझे तू जिस दिन सच में गुजर जाऊँगा
इंतज़ार रहेगा बस उस पल का जब मैं तेरे साथ सारे हदें पार कर जाऊँगा
हो मुश्किलें भले ही समन्दर जितनी
मैं सात समंदर पार कर जाऊँगा
इतना गहरा रिश्ता है मेरा तुझसे
की मैं हर जन्म में तेरा हो जाऊँगा

ना मिले मुझे तू तो मैं पानी सा बन जाऊँगा
बेहता रहूँगा नदियों की तरह और मैं खुद समंदर बन जाऊँगा
इंतज़ार में तेरे मैं बारिश सा बन जाऊँगा
और निकल आये धुप तो मैं बंजर ज़मीन सा बन जाऊँगा
तेरी याद में मैं मुर्झा हुआ फूल बन जाऊँगा
काँटों से होगी मुलाकात और मैं बस पत्थर सा कठोर बन जाऊँगा
होगा जनम फिर तो मैं तेरा आशिक़ बन जाऊँगा
मोहब्बत की गलियों से हर वक़्त गुजर जाऊँगा

HEMA KIRTHIGA J.

She is Hema Kirthiga J., and her pen name is sparkle. She is professionally a psychologist and passionately a writer. She heals others but writing heals her. She is writer, reader, orator and a believer. She is from Chennai. She lives by the principal of inspire and be inspired. She writes her heart and soul and she deeply believe that the depth of her heart and the nib of her pen are soulfully connected. Writing is an art and she is a proud artist. She loves what she does and loves what she writes. Instagram- @the_pen_queen
Email- inker.sparkle@gmail.com Yourquote – JKM

WHO IS SHE?

She is a moon in night,
She is a sun in day,
She is light of dark,
She is a cold in hot,
She is a heat in wind,
She is a magic in this universe,
She is a lover of nature,
She is a fan of birds,
She is looker of sky,
She is as deep as sea,
She is writer in heart,
She is painter in art,
She is the poem in lines,
She faced lots of pains,
She is the one of a kind,
She don't mind,
She never hates,
She never leaves,
She only loves,
Because she is special.

ISHITA TIWARI

A book with a cup of coffee will always be her idea of a perfect evening. Pen and paper are her best friends. The notion of writing with simplicity is her methodology. Besides writing and reading, she loves music.

HOPE AND A REASON TO LIVE

Whatever you do
Whatever you say,
Is all that
Lays in my mind all day.

The way you smile
The way your words carve deep,
Is all that
I dream when I am fast asleep.

Whatever you snap
Whatever you message short or long,
Is all that
I read while listening to that love song.

The way you express
The way those memories you weaved,
Is all that
Gives me hope and a reason to live.

Sunshine

The sun rises
And I look at my phone,
Check the notifications
To see if your messages are shown.

When I find you there
I am the happiest on this Earth,
But when you're not there
I find nothing of any worth.

It feels amazing
When you're online,
And it sucks
When the status shows offline.

I don't know
What to name this obsession of mine,
But all I will say is
You, darling, are my sunshine.

ISHRAT JAHAN NOORMOHAMMED KHAN

Ms. Ishrat Jahan Khan is a passionate teacher and a writer. She loves reading and writing. Loving and caring is her hobby. And keep learning and accept the positive suggestion is her quality. She belongs to North India and stays at Ulhasnagar(Maharashtra). Loves humanity always.

जिंदगी जीने का उमंग

जिंदगी क्या नही समज पाए
खुशियों से ज्यादा दर्द पाए
क्या करे नही समज आता
जब कोई अपना ही करता खता
दोस्त भी दुश्मन निकल रहे
तो दुश्मन से क्या उम्मीद करे
अल्लाह नेमत देता है
अल्लाह ही जिल्लत भी क्यू देता है
मौत आसान बना दो
जिंदगी से मोहब्बत हटा दो
दर्द किसी का कोई बाट नही सकता
हर दर्द की आवाज सबको सुनाई देती है
पर उस दर्द को को दवा नही मिलती है
दुनिया भी बिजी
अपने भी बिजी
सपने सपने तो निजी
निजी बोले तो प्राइवेट बॉक्स में लॉक
जिसे अब कोई नही कर सकता अनलॉक....

ISHRAT SABOON

Ishrat Saboon, from J&K, a passionate writer and a student with classical dreams and vivid wings.

The Leading Road

Sometimes you have to go through
a narrow alley,
In order to avoid the thorns of that
wide track
Don't be surprised, if you are alone!
because living in a herd can never
eliminate the destruction hidden in
the wrong way.

Eternity

When the hope coughs in the battles of life,
and heart surrenders for the bulky roar,
There is a solace in the silence
of a calm soul

JAYASHREE SAHOO

Jayashree Sahoo is habitant of ODISHA. Her writings started on yourquote, notojo and mirakee like writing platforms. You can search her on yourquote by name of Jaya Jayashree. Nowadays, she is member of many writing communities and earned a lot of certificates through her writings.

She is Co-author of 160+ anthologies. Also, she is Compiler of many anthologies in Hindi, English and Odia languages. Currently She is working as project head of a reputed publication. Insta id -@mixing_of_emotions

Email.id- jayashreesahoo665@gmail.com

Feeling of loneliness

Feeling of loneliness
with negative desire, is depression
But feeling of fullness with positive vibes
relaxing the tension.

Decision

Sudden decision creates a new change in life
So, don't take sudden decision in hurry.

KALAMKAAR

This is Kalamkaar. He is from Uttarakhand bought up in Meerut (UP). His hobbies are reading and writing. His interest is in writing. He loves writing. He is part of 295+ Anthologies as Co-Author. He won 290+ Certificates in Writing, He started writing on 29th February 2020. He is part of 2 anthologies as co-author going for record and He is omg record holder as Co -Author of Book Called “Laposia”. He is part of 5 international anthologies as co-author. He is simple and people observer. His insta handle is kalamkaar51 and email is kalamkaar51@gmail.com. He believes in Karma.

पहला प्यार

जब मिलती हैं निगाहे उससे तो सब कुछ धुंदला लगता
हैं !
आती नहीं नींद और खयालो उसके फिर वो जगता है !
जैसे लगता हैं सब कुछ सुहाना हैं !
उसके सिवा नहीं किसी का दिल मे आना हैं !
दिखने के लिए उसको किसी बहाने से उसके घर जाना
हैं !
और होजाता उसका वो दीवाना हैं !
फिर बात करने के लिए किसी बहाने से हिम्मत जुटाना |
फिर हिम्मत करके उससे बात करना, बात करके अपने इश्क़ का
इज़हार करना |
और सातवे आसमान मे ख़ुद को पाना |
जब अपने दिल-o-अज़ीज़ को पा लेना |
उससे सारी बाते करना, उसकी फिक्र जाताना |
उसको प्यार भरे नामो से पुकारना |
अपनी हमेशा पलकों पे बिठाना |
अगर कुछ दफ़े के लिए बात ना करें तो नाराज़गी
जताना |
उसकी मासूमियत पे सब कुछ हार जाना |
नाराज़गी भुलाकर उसको सीने से लगाना |
उसकी पसंद की सारी चीज़े करना !
उसको खोने से डरना !
होता हैं कुछ अलग ही भूत सवार !
ऐसा होता हैं पहला प्यार !

KARAN NISHAD

Karan Nishad, 21 years old from Mumbai. With the dream of exploring the world of his imagination. Also, he is in search of his existence in the world of poetry with some blank pages of his diary.

Simple Things

The beauty in simple things.
Sometimes it's enough
to make us happy.
We forget that simple things,
those little moments
can make a great impact on
our lives and the way we see life.
So, count on the things that matter,
count on the things that make
a positive impact on ourselves.
Simple things make to the
best of the things.

You get me, right?
when I describe you this feeling,
of getting lost, forever,
in the abyss of infinity,
or maybe, of standing alone
at the shore of a lake,
tranquil, still,
with an umbrella black,
you see those stripes of red on it?
They remind me of a distant light,
shining bright in a blackhole.
Yes, perhaps, this is my idea
of PEACE, the eternal peace.
I'm in search of it, the truth is,
we all are in search of it!

KEERTHANA SURIYA

She is Ms. KEERTHANA SURIYA a highly aspired, dynamic medical student, social-worker, a passionate writer and classical dancer who is engaging in self and social development, building relationships and exhibiting integrity. She is co-author of various other anthologies.
She is Founder of WACHC Foundation - Women And Children Health Care and also holding the position of Women's Health Empowerment Project Head in the trust Women's Renaissance Centre.
Follow her on Instagram - @keethusm

ENTHUSIASM IS CONTAGIOUS

You have to be enthusiastic
if you need to feel alive.
You have to be enthusiastic
if you need to enjoy the present moment.
You have to be enthusiastic
if you need to inspire people.
You have to do every task energetically
even if it is a very small task.
Be with people who will encourage you and challenge you to achieve your goals.
If your goals are your seeds
enthusiasm and positivity are the
fertilizers that'll help your seeds grow.
Just like a smile,
enthusiasm is also contagious
Be enthusiastic. Make a difference

KRINJESH MARU

He is a teacher working of the private school, from his age of 16 he started writing quotes shayaris, gazals, currently he is working on a novel which is dedicated to his father.

मै अकेला

तू मेरे खून से मेंहदी रचा ले तुझे हर गुनाह माफ है.
मै गुनेहगार केहलाऊ मंज़ूर है,
सब के ज़ेहन में तो ईमान साफ है ।
कफ़न में लिपटने का मज़ा होगा,
कबर में सोने से सुकून होगा,
इधर मै अकेला हूं , न कोई है ना आप है ।
दूर तक नज़र जाती भी नहीं,
नीचे भी ज़मीं ऊपर भी ज़मीं यहां ना धूप है ना ताप है।
अंधेरा ताबेदार है दोस्त है मेरा ,
शम्मा बुझाओ इससे थोड़ी ख़तरा है ?
अश्क बहाऊ तो कहा बहाऊ ?
हर बूंद में तू है हर बूंद में तेरा सपना है ?
ग़म- ए - ज़िंदगी तुझे कहूं मुनासिब नहीं !
तुभी पराया है, तू कोनसा मेरा अपना है ?
वो सेज़ अभी तक उठाई नहीं है मैंने !
तू लूट किसी और के हाथ,
तुझे अब कोनसा मेरे लिए सजना है !
आखरी ग़ज़ल है जिसमें तेरा ज़िक्र होगा ।
"आज़ाद" को अब कहा तेरे बारे में लिखना है?
मेरा मोल कुछ और है किसी और ने बताया !
मुझे अब कोड़ियो के भाव नहीं बिकना है।
तेरी गली में क्या शहेर में भी नज़र नहीं आऊंगा ।
ना तुझे देखना है ना तुझे दिखना है ।

KRISHNA MOTWANI

Krishna Motwani is a student currently. She uses to pen down her feelings. She is a moody girl. She started writing in the month of June, 2020. She writes in her free time. She writes some motivational quotes or poetries too and practises artwork also. She lives her life like a bird as bird flies freely and enjoys life like that she also lives her life freely and enjoys fullest.
For motivating and inspiring poems and quotes, you can check her on instagram : @ unique__blog_

नारी!

मैं नारी हूं,
अपनी जिंदगी की हर चिंगारी बुझाती हूं।

घर में सब का ख्याल रखती हूं,
मुश्किल वक्त का हंसकर सामना करती हूं।

होते हैं मेरे साथ गंदे काम,
उसके वजह से हो जाती हूं बदनाम।

कोई भेदभाव ना करो मुझ में,
डर सा बैठ गया है मेरे दिल में।

मार देते हो मुझे जन्म लेते ही,
यह याद रखो तुम हो यहां मेरी वजह से ही।

लड़ना पड़े तो लड़ जाऊंगी,
अपनी खुशियां जीत लाऊंगी।

थोड़ा सा हिचकिचाती हूं,
पर हार नहीं मानती हूं।

पूरी दुनिया से लड़ जाऊंगी,
हौसला बुलंद बनाए रखूंगी।

LAXMI MONDAL

Laxmi Mondal is a 17-years-old Science student. She loves writing poems and quotes, it's her passion. She has been a part of an anthology-"Isolating with our minds". She is an aspiring writer.

Till now she had been posting her writings on Instagram @visceral_soul_

MY SHOOTING STAR

It doesn't matter, whether we stay or fall apart
All the moments we spent will be locked in my eyes
I will make your face, with the clouds in the skies
Your name on my lips will stay as pure as a prayer
Even if you hurt me, I will still love you oh I swear
Because you worth it, You worth all the stars
And just to see you, I will go to all the wars.

PEACE

I am glowing in peace, this silence is healing
my heart finally knows, what the hell it is feeling
I am counting my lessons, I am realizing m wrongs
I am living every breath, listening to my songs
The world is on fire, there is only doom they say
but I am finding myself, I am finding my way.

MAUSAM AGRAWAL

She is 22 years old girl from Nepal. She has completed her graduation from Kolkata. She loves to write poems, shayaris and stories.

Chor do mujhko

Tum chor do mujhko
Haan,abb dur ho jao
Jo jhute waade kiye the tumne
Yeh jo jhute kasamein khayi thi
Unhe tum sath le jao
Kisi aur ke kaam aayengi...

Yeh jo yaadein hai tumhari
Jeene nhi deti hai
Na chain se sone deti hai
Ho sake toh unhe bhi apne sath le jao...

Tum chor do mujhko
Haan,abb dur ho jao
Ki tumko paake jo khoya hai
Tum jao par woh lauta jao...

Hoti khata meri
Toh jaana,
Jaan bhi de deta
Yahan toh sab kuch luta ke
Khatao se anjaan hun..

Tum chor do mujhko
Haan,dur ho jao
Ki yeh jo baatein hai tumhari yeh abb bardast nahi hoti..

MOHANAPRIYA K.

Co-author Mohanapriya K. is a good writer from Tamilnadu, India. She has completed her Bachelor's degree in Engineering stream. She has been a writer for one year as her passion. She wants to be a best compiler and curator in future. She will try to express what comes to her mind through her words as it is. For her writing is a great art. The art of giving pleasure to the mind and helping to forget the worries in the mind. She is very happy to undertake such noble art. Yet she sincerely hopes that this writing journey of her will continue sweetly as is now and will bring her many successes.

The emotions we carry

Some emotions are always within us and we cannot hide them even though we think we should hide them.
What could be a creature without emotions!
In this, heartfelt emotions are very important and essential.
Because many of us are walking the path of our heart, living by accepting what our heart says as scripture and as the master of our conscience.
We should never underestimate the fact that we burn ourselves out for certain things because the vehicle is running because the fuel in the vehicle is burning.
There is no vehicle without fuel and fuel is like life to that vehicle.
Burning ourselves within ourselves will solidify us.

The positive thoughts we have on ourselves

The beauty of the broken wing is that it bears so much pain and we break in the same way Only the wings have been shown solely to give a sense of proportion.
Just because we have the crown in our hands does not mean that we are the king or queen, it is that he has made us king and queen?
Instead of being a king/queen from such a crown we can be just an ordinary person.
It is normal to look for light in a dark place but how can we find light in that dark life by completely darkening our own life, rather than wandering in search of light after dark, I am the one who seeks the right light in the light of false darkness and darkness is always greater to me than the lamp that gives false light.

OM PRAKASH LOVEVANSHI

उनका जन्म राजस्थान के बाराँ जिले के गाँव देहलनपुर में हुआ। उनकी उम्र 24 साल हैं। उनकी रचनायें मासिक पत्रिकाओं और 50 से अधिक साझा काव्य संग्रहों में प्रकाशित हुई हैं। उन्होने कोटा विश्वविद्यालय से हिंदी साहित्य में ग्रेजुएशन किया। अभी वर्धमान खुला विश्वविद्यालय से हिंदी भाषा में पोस्ट ग्रेजुएशन कर रहे हैं। उनकी साहित्य में रूचि है।

अकेले चलो

जब कोई भी तुम्हारा साथ ना दे
तब तुम अकेले चलो
खुद नया रास्ता बनाओ
और उस पर निरंतर चलो
थकना नहीं है रुकना नहीं है।
तुम एक न एक दिन
मंजिल जरूर पाओगे
और फिर लोग चलेंगे,
तुम्हारे बनाए उन्हीं रास्तों पर
जिन पर चलकर तुम आगे बढ़े हो।
तुम्हारे कदमों के निशानों पर
कदम रखकर आगे बढ़ेंगे
और आखिर वो भी पा जायेंगे मंजिल।।

PRAGYA VERMA

Pragya Verma hails from Prayagraj, Uttar Pradesh. She is a poetess and a writer. She has done 75+ anthologies, and two international anthologies and currently doing two world record anthologies as a co-author. She is also compiling two anthologies named, "SHADES OF NIGHT" & "In A Relationship With Success". She has a great interest in making paintings and doing photography. She loves to gain spiritual knowledge and tries to find peace everywhere.
You can follow her on Instagram @wordsofpragya

Heart Over Mind

This head is full of darkness,
That gave me unwanted sadness.
It gives me depression and overthinking,
And in this I feel like I'm sinking, I'm sinking.
Here, I have my heart,
It shows me a way to new start.
That gave me love and peace,
It beats in all of its broken piece,
I take decision with my heart,
Sometimes, this mind becomes too dark.
Maybe my decision come out wrong,
Maybe I have to deal with my head's storm,
But in all of this, my heart kept me strong,
That made this cold heart once again warm.

इश्क की कलम

इश्क की कलम चल पड़ी है,
अपनी स्याही से कुछ लिख रही है।
एक नई प्रेम कहानी रची है,
जिसमें छुपी दिलों की खुशी है।
हर रोज़ कितनी ही कहानी रचती है,
हर पल दो दिलों को मिलाती है।
तेरी स्याही कभी खत्म न होती,
यह कैसी जादूगरी है?
कितने ही दिल आशिकी में पड़े हैं,
अंजान होते हुए भी दिल से जुड़े हैं।
ऐ कलम, तुम लिखो कई कहानी,
मगर मंज़िल भी लिखो उन कहानियों की।
जिसमें न बिखरे, न टूटे यह दिल,
इश्क को दो तुम एक ऐसी मंज़िल।

PRAGYAN PANDA

Pragyan is pursuing her B.Tech in "Chemical Engineering" from IGIT, Sarang. She's a short girl from Rourkela, Odisha. With fascination of nature, she's a spiritual person who motivates people. She does weird stuff like interacting with non living ones and pens down her mind.
For more of her works, do follow her IG @quote_love_97

GUILT

The regular frustrating guilt;
The darkest black hue just to escape light.
It's when realization strike too late but kills;
Much audible like the scary cries of the dying zeals.
The scents of the corpse flower or rotten dihydrogen sulphide in labs:
Signifying the ultimate give ups to cheap guilts and pure stagnation by losing dignity.

PRASAD BABU GALLA

Prasad Babu Galla, is 30 years old and belongs to Visakhapatnam. He pursued bachelor's degree and aims to become a successful author. He is making efforts in finding out more opportunities to get the best out of him. He started writing to express his thoughts from his heart and now he debuted as a co-author of anthologies. He loves writing about Love and Inspirational Stories.

To reach him, you can contact on his personal Instagram handle @prasadbabugalla
Your Quote @prasadbabugalla
Email id:- babuprasad20@gmail.com

You are My Everything

You are my sun that shine throughout my day.
You are my moon that glint throughout my night.
You are my star that gleam so bright.
You are my everything.

You are my heart that beats inside.
You are my blood that flows through me.
You are my oxygen that I live my breath.
You are my everything.

You are my one and only.
You are my wife, I am your hubby
You never stop me from being so lonely.
You are my everything.

You are my future like a glue.
I never want to lose you.
I want to be with you for the rest of my life.
You are my everything.

PRATIK JADHAV

He is hailing from the city Terkheda, Osmanabad. He is pursuing his degree in Pharmacy Education. He loves to write what's in his mind. He wishes to nurture his poetry more and more in upcoming days.

शेतकऱ्यांची व्यथा

निसर्ग कोपला,
देवही झोपला
हक्कासाठी तो दिल्लीतही पोहचला.
झुंजावे कोणाशी लढावे कोणाशी,
आपलेच खेळतात खेळ आपल्याशी.
ज्याची भाकर त्यालाच नाही,
"बड्यांची" झोळी मात्र भरलेलीच राही.
काय केलं होत वाईट त्याने
उठलात त्याच्या जीवावर,
आणून ठेवले हे जीव घेणे
कायदे त्याच्या उरावर.
आत्महत्या ही केली त्याने
धरले नाही जबाबदार कोणाला,
हे सारं काही कळूनही
किंचितही फरक पडला नाही "बड्यांच्या" मनाला.
अरे "बड्या" असं वागणं सोडून दे,
माणूस म्हणून त्याला जगून दे.

बस इतनी सी राहत है

पता है मिल नहीं सकते
मगर खत भेजकर हाल पूछते हो
बस इतनी सी राहत है।
तुम तो साथ नहीं हो
मगर तुम्हारी याद साथ है
बस इतनी सी राहत है।
नसीब में हो या नहीं मालूम नहीं
मगर जहन में सिर्फ तुम हो
बस इतनी सी राहत है।
हमें अभी पता चला है की
मन्नते करते हो तुम हमारी
बस इतनी सी राहत है।
बस इतनी सी राहत है की,
मुसीबत में साथ देकर
हौसला बढ़ाते हो,
तुम ही तो हो
जो मुझे जिंदगी बताते हो।

PUNITA SINHA

Punita Sinha considers herself a learner and an observer and her first love to be music and words. She isn't good at telling out loud her feelings therefore, she writes. She's someone who can travel miles alone only if she's earphones on, a camera of any sort to capture and something to write upon.

WRONG PEOPLE

I saw you last day laughing
But you don't laugh anymore
Just the people annoy you
Or it's the whole world
You think you're broken
Not ever to be mend
But don't you see
You're more stronger than them

They break you and leave you
You wait for them
They take your peace and health
And tell all of it's, you began
You try to bring them back
And love them as you never before
But tell me, luv
Do they deserve any of these
When they already left you
And left you to rot ashore

Let me tell you a secret
This is not your real happiness
The person who leaves you are
Just mere because of their emptiness
And let me tell you one another thing
You'll live and laugh like never before
You just need to be free from such souls
And I promise you'll receive much more
Greater things and people than now
And not more of any such cripples
Because darling, you're not weak
You just came across wrong people!

RAHUL SHENDE

Rahul Satyawan Shende
Poet and writer
College student
A/p - Telangwadi
Tal - Mohol
Dist – Solapur

भारताची गौरवगाथा

हाडाचा हिंदुस्थानी मी
ठेवतो भारत मातेच्या चरणी माथा
15 ऑगस्ट स्वातंत्र्य दिनी
गातो मी भारताची गौरवगाथा

जन्म दिला एकीने
थारा दिला एकीने
आज आभार मानू त्या मायेचे
चला ऋण फेडू भारतमातेचे

हिऱ्या सारखी माणसे आमुची
सोन्यासारखे माती
आठवता इतिहास पूर्वजांचा
फुगते 56 इंच छाती

अभिमान वाटतो
इथे जन्मल्याचा
गर्व आहे मला
मी हिंदुस्थानी असल्याचा.

विठु माझा सावळा

पंढरीचा पांडुरंग
विठू माझा सावळा
डोक्यावरती सोन्याचा मुकुट
मस्तकी चंदनाचा टिळा
33 कोटी देवा मध्ये
विठू माझा सावळा

सोनेरी बाजूबंद दंडावरती
त्याला मोत्यांची वाळा
विटेवरी उभा घेऊन तुळशी माळा गळा पंढरीचा स्वामी विठु माझा सावळा

सोन्याची पंढरी तशी
रुक्मिणी स्वर्गाची सुंदरी
तिला शोभून दिसे विठोबा काळा
रुक्मिणीचा पती विठू माझा सावळा

भक्तांचा लाडका विठु माझा सावळा
विठू माझा सावळा.

REENA KADAM

Reena Chetan Kadam from Maharashtra. She is a good writer. She believes herself as a born poetess. She loves to write and express in her own way and also have a talent of singing. She is aiming to persuade her dream to write a series of her poetry.

केसांचा पिंजरा

हळुवार त्या गालावरून केसांची बट सळसळत होती
त्या घनदाट केसांची वेणी त्याला मोहित करत होती
हलकेच सुटलेल्या त्या केसांच्या झुपकेत धावत येऊन तो सामवायचा
आणि तो निघुन जाऊ नये म्हणुन मीच त्याला त्या केसांच्या पिंजरेत बांधून ठेवत होती
पण अचानक एके दिवशी त्या गालावरून सळसळणारी ती बट नाहीशी झाली होती
आरशात पाहिलं तर पायाखालची जमीनच सरकली होती
कंगव्याचा स्पर्श सुद्धा त्या टाळूला जाणवत न्हवता
जरा जोराने केस विंचरावे म्हटलं तर केसातली जट किंकाळ्या फोडत होती
नंतर आठवलं मी तर त्याला माझ्या केसांच्या पिंजऱ्यात बांधून ठेवलं होतं
म्हणून हातानेच एक एक जट सोडवत होती
घाईघाईने घेतला तर होता तो केसांचा गुंतावळा सोडवायला
ऽपण त्या निर्दयी जटांनी त्याची आस तिथेच संपवली होती

REETIKA SINGH

This is Reetika Singh. Born in Mokama, Bihar in 2001. She is 19 and currently pursuing B.com Honors with CMA USA at Graphic Era Deemed to be University. She has completed her diploma in Karate Shotokan 1st Dan. She has a versatile nature and calm mind. Besides writing she is a virtual artist also.

Disconsolate

Do you ever wake up in the middle of the night and just think about where you thought you were gonna be at this point in life?
I said no to a lot of things the world has told me
I'm supposed to say yes to.
I lost a lot of things I really thought I needed.
You always end up where you are supposed to be.
Even if it hurts a lot getting there.

IT'S ALWAYS WORTH IT.

Rishte

Rishte hawa ki tarah hone chaiye,
Khamosh magar aas paas.

Jindagi

Kirdaar, kahani sab mitt jayega,
Tu aaj ji le kal jindagi ka waqt bitt jayega.

Buckets

Karwi magar sachi baat,
Jab khud ko chot lagti h tabhi dusro ki dikhayi deti hai.

RESHMA ANWAR SHAIKH

Reshma Anwar Shaikh currently pursuing her degree in Economics at Dhempe College Of Arts and Science. She loves to express her feelings through words. She is a proud NCC Cadet. She loves to travel. She is the President of HKGN self help group in Chimbel-Goa. She loves to try different cuisines as well.

MY SOULMATE

Mother you've given me so much,
love from your heart and warmth of your touch.

The love you give so honest and pure
Keeping me forever safe and secure
There's no love like a mother's
Her heart is filled with care.

A mother's love is something that
No one can explain,
It is made up with deep sacrifice and pain.

There is no other creation like mother
It is rarest in the world
It believes beyond believing
When the world around condemns.

The one that's always been there,
Right from the start.
With all love, hope and care
You taught me from your heart.

SAHINA GHUGHA

Sahina Ghugha is 20-year-old B.Com student at Saurashtra University Rajkot. She is from Jamnagar city of Gujarat. She is state level winner in poetry competition 2017. She is Co-author of 10+ anthologies. She is an amazing writer and poet and she wants do something for society through her pen.
Insta ID: - @Itz_Sahina_write

वैसा ही ख़्वाब

अंधेरों में देता सुकून जो, तू वैसा ही ख़्वाब है
आंखें छलकता जाम, मुस्कुराहट तेरी शराब है

यूं मिले है हम भी कई खूबसूरत बलाओ से
पर जो अच्छाई तुझ में है, वो सबसे खराब है

तू भले ही मुंह मोड़ ले, सच्चाई तो बदलेगी नहीं
इश्क़ तुझे भी है हम से, ये बात ही शबाब है

इश्क़ हमारे को दे दो चाहे नाम एक पागलपन का,
जो शीशा है अपने प्यार का, इसमें ना दरार है

राग जो मैं गाता जाऊं, तेरी तारीफ़ कभी कम नहीं
आंखें छलकता जाम, मुस्कुराहट तेरी शराब है

SAUMYA BHATIA

Saumya Bhatia is a 21-year-old, Delhi girl. She is currently pursuing her post-graduation. She started writing as a hobby and now this hobby is slowly and gradually developing into passion. She aspires to be a writer. She wants to reach to people's heart through her writing.

शायरी

गलती है हमारी,
जो सच समझ बैठे,
मज़ाक किआ था तुने,
हम अपना हक समझ बैठे,
बस इज़हार किआ तब तुमने,
हम प्यार समझ बैठे।

खोया हुँ, रोया हुँ,
तेरी बेरुखी सह सह के सोया हुँ,
हार के बैठता तो हुँ कभी,
और फिर भी, मैं उठता हुँ।

कोई मुझे समझ नहीं पाता,
लेकिन क्यों? सबका सब कुछ मुझे समझ आता,
कोई मुझे पढ़ नहीं पाता,
लेकिन क्यों? सबकी आँखें मेरी नज़रो में नज़र आता,
कोई मेरे साथ खड़ा रह नहीं पाता,
लेकिन क्यों? सबके साथ मैं होती हुँ ,
मेरे साथ कोई रह नहीं पाता।

जो भी आपके लिए अच्छा है,
उसका फैसला आपका रब करता है,
जो भी आपके लिए बुरा है,
उसको अच्छा करने की ज़िम्मेदारी,
आपके रब की है।

मेरे भाग्य की लकीरें,
गहरी बहुत है,

बनाती और बदलती खुद हुँ इनको,
अपने ज़ोर से।

नया दौर आएगा,
नई बाहार लाएगा,
वो सड़को का शोर फिर होगा,
बच्चो के खेल की पुकार फिर होगी,
साथ वाली आंटी के साथ,
एक बार फिर गप- शप लगाएंगे,
हम सब, नया दौर लाएंगे।

SHAZIA JABEEN

Name: Shazia Jabeen
Anthologies: so many
Studying: high school
Institute: Sri Chaitanya techno curriculum
She loves reading, writing.

Enthusiasm

Boost your energy level. If you're a quiet, introverted person, you don't have to pretend you're outgoing and "bubbly". ...
Ask a lot of questions. ...
When something sounds interesting, say so. ...
Compliment them. ...
Perfect your posture. ...
Finish strong!

Thinking about Bad Things is enough to make anyone serious. But when you're enthusiastic, importance translates into passion – and the whole thing becomes fun. There are few things more enjoyable than talking enthusiastically about something you're passionate about, and feeling others share your enthusiasm.

"You will do foolish things, but do them with enthusiasm." ...
"Some of us get dipped in flat, some in satin, some in gloss...."
He turned to me. ...
"Live your truth. ...
"I began to realize how important it was to be an enthusiast in life. ...
"Enthusiasm can help you find the new doors, but it takes passion to open them.

It's your life; live it well." ...

"Let your dreams be bigger than your fears, your actions louder than your words, and your faith stronger than your feelings." ...
"We don't meet people by accident. ...

"Taking care of yourself makes you stronger for everyone in your life … ...

"Negative people need drama like it's oxygen....

How can we increase my energy and enthusiasm?

By sleeping well, eating well, reducing your stress levels and exercising you will have higher energy. You can bring passion to your days with more energy which leads to greater enthusiasm. Never give up: In order to maintain your enthusiasm going with high energy you need to make the decision to never give up.

SHIVANGI PATANKAR

Shivangi Patankar is a young girl from Mumbai, Maharashtra who is fond of writing. She completed her graduation from Mumbai University. She has interest in writing on topics based on regional, relation, social etc. specially in her mother tongue Marathi.

She has her Instagram account named @Kavya_marathi28

आयुष्याची परीक्षा

प्रगतीच्या मार्गात लाख येतील अडचणी
माणसानं लढत राहावं न जाता खचूनी

न डगमगता त्यानं संकटाला सामोरं जावं
अन् त्यातून जमेल तसं शिकून ही घ्यावं

करत असताना प्रगती चढावी लागेल कधी अपयशाची पायरी
पण त्यानंतर मिळेल जे यश त्याची असेल बातच काही न्यारी

म्हणे सहजासहजी मिळालेली कोणतीच गोष्ट टिकत नाही
अन् सहज मिळालेल्या गोष्टीची तसंही माणसांना किंमतच नसते काही

आयुष्यात घडणारी प्रत्येक गोष्ट काही ना काही शिकवून जाते आपल्याला
अन् त्यातूनच नवी उमेद अन् हिंमत मिळते लढायला

सहज मार्गाने मिळणाऱ्या यशा पेक्षा कधीही चांगलं अपयश
त्यातूनच शिकलेल्या गोष्टी आयुष्यात उपयोगी पडतात मिळवताना यश

मेहनत करावी माणसानं न ठेवता फळाची अपेक्षा
अन् हिंमत करून द्यावी आयुष्याची ही परीक्षा

नाती

जपावी लागतात नाती विसरून सारं काही
रुसवे फुगवे धरून मुळी चालतच नाही

ऐकून घ्यावं लागतं सगळ्यांचं गप राहून
उलट बोलून कोणाला मुळी चालतच नाही

विश्वासावरच नाती टिकतात सारी
अविश्वास दाखवून नात्यात मुळी चालतच नाही

जपावी लागतात लहान थोर साऱ्यांची मनं
तोडून मन कोणाचं मुळी चालतच नाही

नात्यातला गोडवा हळूवार उलगडण्यात असतो
घाई करुन नात्यात मुळी चालतच नाही

SHIVANI BHARDWAJ

keep going

Paramedical student, melophile.

SIGN ANY CONTRACT: -when we are completely in relationship.

"Relationship" not means only for boys and girls it means friendship b/w the humans. Actually, you like their companies and can be say want to be more time and spend it.
Some people say this is 'love'.
What is love????
Love is that where we want to share own thoughts, spending time, enjoy freely live with them makes you feel special in your lifestyle, and always remember that someone with me not behind in my life journey. And it called to be perfect understanding between the couples....
When you're really engrossed in your own world and you are just predicament situation and not be part become any type enthusiasm moments with them.
Because you are so serious about their responsibilities.
When you know that "you are just made for each other".
Relationship/ love is a contract yeah deal where we have sign and give the any commit, to share the feelings, to each other when we ain't reluctant not feel comfortable for sharing because you don't want to see them in panic situation.
If you love someone truly you will hardly try to understand his / her emotions and help in expedition of their life's but sometimes need to be patience situation are different in your relationship without saying a thin.
When you fall in love with someone you will be spell bound his voice and literally addicted to listen them voice and try to saying everything in lucid manner.
"When we committed with someone, we have not signed any contract for learning but you learn to control your jealousy, you put mock smile on your face, conscience, stop yourself to do cheesy mistake, control your aggravated behavior,

sometime we have to take decision that type protect our existence.....
Seriously we have dealt in love.
You will put their happiness above yours. You want the best for them otherwise they broke up....?
Sometimes we killing our best ever feelings for someone.....
Love is contract.

SHRADHA GINDLANI

Shradha Gindlani is from a small town with big dreams taking hold of her heart and brain, day and night. With a vision of community to serve those in need of education and literacy she aspires high. She writes poetries and prose mainly. She is kind hearted and helping personality indeed.

मेरी उमंग की उड़ान

मेरे छोटे छोटे कदम
उनकी छलांग से डरते है

वो अपनी हदो का बिछोना
मेरे अस्तित्व के उपर ढकते है

आँखें शक के दलदल से भरी
मुझे बार बार रोकती है

पर मेरी उमंग की उड़ान ऊचि देख
अब वो खुद पर ही हस्ते है।

SIDDHI SHRIKRISHNA KULKARNI

She is Miss Siddhi Shrikrishna Kulkarni, completed BSc agriculture. She has much more interest in poetry and also in writing, speaking, reading and anchoring. She did very well.

विश्वंभर

|| तूची विश्वंभर तूची सर्व त्राता
ठाई ठाई भक्तांच्या तू
चरणी आज माथा..
आला कसोटीचा काळ..
तरी तू पाठीशी खंबीर..
आज जरी तू पंढरपुरी
तरी मनी भरुनी उरलासी..
पोलिसांच्या रूपाने तू रक्षिलेस जना..
वैद्यांच्या रूपाने जीवदान दिले जना..
बळीराजा करवी पोट भरले तू जगाचे
तूच कृपावंत तूच आभाळ माऊली..
कसं पांग फेडू सांग सावळे विठाई...||

नीरव शांतता

लुकलुकत्या रात्री सांभाळत रोजचा चंद्र सजत आहे..
कधी कोर कधी पूर्ण..
खेळ लपंडाव खेळतो आहे..
तोच चंद्रमा नभात..
रोज नवी छटा सोडतो आहे..
तुझ्या सोबतीने निरव शांतता ही होते हळवी..
अन् ओठांवर उगा रेंगाळीती ओळी..
तुझा शीतल प्रकाश जशी खळी खुले गाली
मग वारा हलकेच फुंकर घाली..
मन मोहरुन जाई..मन मोहरुन जाई..

SHRIJANI DAS

Currently studying in class 11, favorite hobbies include reading and writing.

The Prey

She is always at defense
Her first instinct is never offence
The animal goes away doing his deed
Sowing away it's disgusting seed of greed
She is still in pain and Horror
Even if the deed was done long prior
Still living in that dreadful moment
She finds herself uncomfortable even covered in many layers of garment
Sees her future breaking down in her mind
Dreads herself for being kind
Once filled with light, joy and positiveness
Is now reduced to void, despair and negativeness
Only a few minutes were taken
To make her see that her spotless reflection is broken
Always fighting to preserve her innocence and values
She finds herself at the moment without any clues

TANMAY YADAV

Tanmay Yadav is a resident from Mumbai who likes writing shayaris. He has a deeper interest in cricket.
Presently he is trying to get settled and likes to write what he feels in the form of shayaris.

तेरी हसी।

सुबह की पहली किरन की तरह,
रोनक लाती है तेरी हसी।।
शाम के रंगीन मौसम की तरह,
प्यार सा भर देती है तेरी हसी।।
तेरी अदा ही कुछ ऐसी है मेरी जान।।
दिन भर की थकान,
निकाल देती है तेरी हसी।।

दोस्ती।

चाहे सुख में तेरे साथ ना हो,
दुख में तेरा सहारा बने रहेंगे हम।।
तू कोई मुश्किल तो बता दे,
उसका हल धुंदने निकलेंगे हम।।
यू तो इस रिश्ते को कई नाम दिए है,
लेकिन एक दूसरे का हात कभी ना छोड़ेंगे हम।।

ये आशिकी

उनकी फितरत तो है,
आखों से बिजली गिराने की।।
वहीं हरमी ज़िद है,
उन बिलजियो को सहने की।।
यू तो कई घायल हुए है,
इनकी अदाओं के चलते।।
लेकिन हमारी कोशिश तो है,
उनकी आशिकी हासिल करने की।।

खूप काही सांगायचं होतं

खूप दिवसान पासून सांगायचं होत,
मनातलं तुझ्याशी बोलायचं होत...
का कुणास ठाऊक जमलं नाही मला,
घरच्यान समोर हात तुझा धरून बसायचं होत....
ती वेळ कधी येईल ठाऊक नाही मला,
आयुष्यभर प्रेमात तुझा राहायचं होत....
का कुणास ठाऊक जमलं नाही मला,
हेच तुला आता सांगायचं होत...

UTKARSH DEVALE

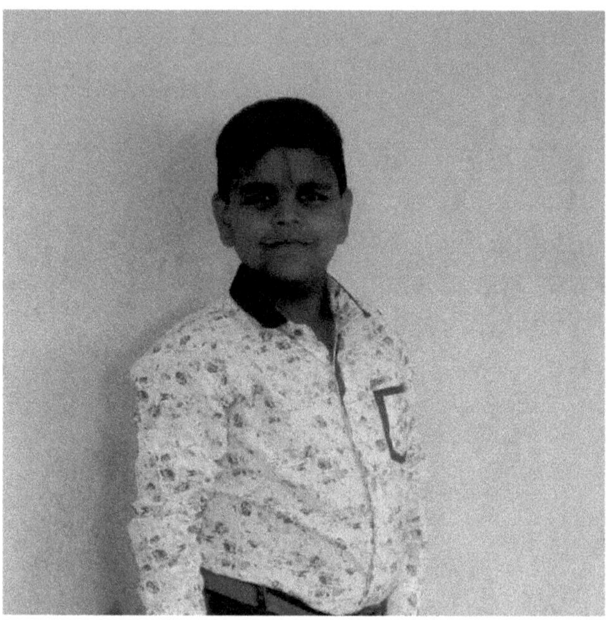

He is a student learning in the Seventh standard. He is fond of learning new science experiments along with sketching also. Sometimes he tries to express himself in the poetic words. He is hailing from the holy city, Pandharpur.

उमेद

सकारात्मक विचारांशिवाय आपुले जीवन अपूर्णच जणु! प्रत्येकाला जीवनात किमान एकदा तरी नैराश्य, हार यांस सामोरे जावेच लागते. आपल्यामध्ये असणाऱ्या इच्छाशक्तीच्या जोरावर माणूस नव्याने उभा राहतो. पुन्हा एकदा उमेदीने जीवन जगून आयुष्यात आलेला अंधार दूर करू शकतो.

आपल्या विचारांवरती जर आपले नियंत्रण असेल तरच आपण सकारात्मक बदल घडवून आणू शकतो. केवळ नकारात्मक विचार करणे हा मनुष्यगुण आहे, या निर्णयावर तर आपला द्रृष्टीकोन अथवा व्यवहार अवलंबून असतो! विशेषतः आपण जसा विचार करतो, तसेच बनत जातो! त्यामुळे सकारात्मक रहा, नव्या उमेदीने कामाला लागा !!

VAISHNAVI HEND

Vaishnavi Hend lives in the orange city- Nagpur. She is a creator by habit, a microbiologist by occupation and an amateur writer by her choice. She is conceptual and curious to create herself. She loves to create, communicate and share her thoughts with her poetry and writings. You can get to me by typing Blink2Think-B2T on YouTube.

Sense of Excitement

In the journey of our life,
We do lots of work, we learn lots of things
There are some habits, relationships or activities that don't work for us…
Instead of working on it, we simply leave them out of our life
We blame things for that, which actually don't link…
But, it's important to grow in you the sense of excitement, don't you think..?
We have one life to grow ourselves and to know ourselves
Experiencing a life with all your experiences is great
But, experience without excitement is like a calendar without any date…
Think of the days, when you were a kid
Each and every work with full of interest and excitement you did…
Success, satisfaction and happiness are interlinked…
But, it's important to grow in you the sense of excitement, don't you think..?
It's important to have someone to love and experience that
But, the relationship without excitement is a boring act
In every relationship we are involved,
Whether it's he or she, male or female, blue or pink...
But, it's important to grow in you the sense of excitement, don't you think..?
We lose the possibilities of the idea of excitement without any imagination
It's a dream in the world of visualization and creation…
Excitement boosts the power in us
So, don't let your excitement to shrink or sink
Because it's important to grow in you the sense of excitement,
Just Blink and Think…

VINOD UMRATKAR

हे विनोद उमरतकर आहेत, ते कळंब (यवतमाळ) येथे राहतात, त्यांना लिहायला आवडते, खासकरून त्याच्या कविता नावानुसार विनोदी असतात, ते जिप यवतमाळ येथे ग्रामसेवक म्हणून कार्यरत आहेत.

रंग रांगोळीचे

रंग रांगोळीचे।
झालेत बेरंग।
तुझा तो रंग।
वगळता।।
फुलझडी माझी।
बसली रूसून।
नाक फुगवून।
माझ्यावरी।।
तूच जर सखे।
असेल नाराज।
दिव्यांची आरास।
कशी करू।।
सोड ना रुसवा।
आता तरी राणी।
गाऊ दीप गाणी।
संगतीने।।
चल काढू सखे।
रांगोळी रंगाची।
सुखी संसाराची।
रंगवूनी।।

Flairs and Glairs, a platform by a student for the students. We are esteemed youth struggling to carve out our path for our future and we follow a basic mindset Since everyone is not born with all-round skills. Joining hands with people who are born to execute it with perfection is the best way to evolve. Self-Evolution is the need of the hour but, evolving as a community is what we strive for. The initiative as kickstarted by, Founder- Mr. Shubham Shah with the motive to utilize the skillset and talent of writing has now a team of 10+ people who are actively participating into newer forms of learning and discovering talents among youngsters. We Provide platform and services like Publishing opportunities, Open mics, Workshops, Hands-on training. Operating with Brand Name of Flairs and Glairs (Publication House), we offer the chance of elevating a passionate writer to an esteemed author With Brand name Teekhe Zasbaaat. We bring to you an opportunity to get accustomed with the Public Speaking and Presenting of Thoughts along with regular challenges to brush up your inking spirit. The newest initiative to extend our services we introduced in a new writing Platform- The Glittering Fables and Ink Over Tears.

We Choose to Fly Like A Falcon than to be a Leg Pulling Crab.

www.ingramcontent.com/pod-product-compliance
Ingram Content Group UK Ltd.
Pitfield, Milton Keynes, MK11 3LW, UK
UKHW022005190726
13853UKWH00004B/1744